This book belongs to:

_____

Mama's Many Hats

To: Sallie~
Many Blessings
to my fellow author!
Keep writing & follow your dreams!
Lorie A. Erhard
~ 2015

written by
Lorie Erhard

illustrated by
Jennifer Kalis

BUMBLE BEE BOOKS

For my three busy bumblebees, Ryan, Tyler, and Brooke, who introduced me to my many hats!
I'm so thankful for you! You fill my hat boxes with joy!

For my mom, Louise, who wears the hats of encouragement and compassion so beautifully.
You are a wonderful grandmother and a good friend. Grandma would be so proud!

Many thanks to my loving family and friends who have been a great encouragement in the making of this book.
Hats off to you! I adore you all!

And, special thanks to God, the Creator of all good things and all good hats! - L.E.

Thanks to my mom and dad, for their unconditional love of their grandchildren. - J.K.

Published by Bumble Bee Books
Champaign, Illinois
Bumble-Bee-Books.com

Lorie A. Erhard, Author
Jennifer Kalis, Illustrator

Illustration Ideas: Jennifer Kalis & Lorie Erhard
    with special suggestions from Brooke Erhard & Tyler Erhard
Contributing Editor: Ryan Erhard
Book Layout: Jennifer Kalis

Scripture quotations marked (NIV) are taken from the Holy Bible, New International Version®, NIV®.
Copyright © 1973, 1978, 1984, 2011 by Biblica, Inc.™ Used by permission of Zondervan. All rights reserved worldwide. www.zondervan.com. The "NIV" and "New International Version" are trademarks
registered in the United States Patent and Trademark Office by Biblica, Inc.™

Scripture quotations marked (NLT) are taken from the Holy Bible, New Living Translation, copyright © 1996, 2004, 2007, 2013 by Tyndale House Foundation. Used by permission of Tyndale House
Publishers, Inc., Carol Stream, Illinois 60188. All rights reserved.

Scripture quotations marked (NCV) are quoted from The Holy Bible, New Century Version®, copyright © 1987, 1988, 1991 by Word Publishing, a division of Thomas Nelson, Inc. Used by permission.

Library of Congress Control Number: 2014931968

ISBN 978-0-9914701-4-3

~First Edition

Summary: Mama wears her many hats with thankfulness and joy as she lovingly shares them with her children, ultimately, sharing God's love with the world!

Printed in Mexico on acid-free paper

Hi Kidzzz!

Are you ready to have some fun?

"Bee" on the lookout for the following things throughout the story:

 A busy little bumblebee doing something silly on each page!

Clues to help you figure out what hat Mama's wearing next!

 Mama's camera throughout the story!

And, after you buzz through the story, there are some fun activities for you to do at the end!

So put on your thinking caps, turn on your antennae, and get buzzing!

Joyfully,
Lorie Erhard

My mama likes to wear her sparkly jewels
Snazzy shoes and frilly scarves
But wearing her many treasured hats
Shows the love inside her heart

Luke 12:34 "Wherever your treasure is, there the
desires of your heart will also be." (NLT)

My mama wears a BIRTHDAY HAT
Throughout each day of the year
Daily, she celebrates Christ's birth
And she knows He's always near

Luke 1:14 "You will have great joy and gladness,
and many will rejoice at his birth..." (NLT)

My mama wears a NURSE'S CAP
When I fall and scrape my knee
And when I'm feeling feverish
She takes good care of me

Psalm 30:2 "O Lord my God, I called to you for help,
and you healed me." (NIV)

My mama wears a CHEF'S HAT
When she cooks yummy food galore
She makes it all with her special touch
And I always come back for more

My mama must wear a HALO
When she saves me from danger and harm
I'm certain she's my guardian angel
So I can feel safe and unalarmed

Psalm 40:11 "....may your love and your truth always protect me." (NIV)

My mama wears a PIONEER'S HAT
When she tells stories of long ago
I'm so glad I'm in God's family
And in love and faith, I'll grow

1 John 3:1 "See how very much our Father
loves us, for he calls us his children,
and that is what we are!" (NLT)

My mama wears a MAID'S HAT
Making our home fresh and tidy each day
She helps me grow a pure, clean heart
And says, God washes my sins away

Psalm 51:10 "Create in me a pure heart, O God,
and renew a steadfast spirit within me. (NIV)

My mama wears a PILOT'S HAT
Steering me eagerly toward my dreams
Cuz God wants me to do great things
And in His plans for me, she beams

Jeremiah 29:11 "For I know the plans I have for you," says the Lord.
"They are plans for good ... to give you a future and a hope." (NLT)

My mama wears a FRENCH BERET
When we paint with colors in every shade
She says I'm God's artistic masterpiece
Beautifully and wonderfully made

Psalm 139:14 "I praise you because you made me in an amazing and wonderful way." (NCV)

My mama wears a RAIN HAT
On days when I'm feeling sad
She pours out stories of God's promises
So I feel warm, encouraged, and glad

Jeremiah 31:13 "...I will give them comfort
and joy instead of sorrow." (NIV)

Mama wears a JACK-IN-THE-BOX HAT
When she plans many a fun surprise
She can make an ordinary day quite special
By bringing laughter-n-joy to my eyes

Luke 11:13 "So if you...know how to give good gifts
to your children, how much more will your heavenly
Father give the Holy Spirit to those who ask him." (NLT)

My mama wears a COWBOY HAT
As we gallop toward good deeds
We round up extra food and clothes
To care for others' needs

Hebrews 13:16 "And do not forget to do good
and to share with others,
for with such sacrifices God is pleased." (NIV)

My mama wears a COACH'S HAT
Both on and off the green
Guiding me to do my best and be fair
Cuz Jesus is there with me

Philippians 4:13 "For I can do everything through Christ,
who gives me strength." (NLT)

SAFARI
GOLF
#3

My mama wears a SAFARI HAT
Leading the way through exciting adventures
We set up camp and hike through God's woods
With our pup and butterfly catchers

Genesis 1:1 "In the beginning God created the heavens and earth." (NIV)

My mama wears a MINER'S HAT
When she tip-toes through the night
She prays for me and tucks me in
Keeping me cozy till morning's light

Psalm 145:20 "The Lord watches over
all who love him..." (NIV)

My mama wears a TOP HAT
When we feel like goofing around
We sing, dance, laugh, and praise
Filling our home with joyful sounds

Psalm 100:1-2 "Shout with joy to the Lord, all the earth.
Worship the Lord with gladness;
come before him with joyful songs." (NIV)

My mama wears a POSTAL CAP
When she delivers to me good news
She tucks surprises inside my lunchbox
For me and my friends too

Romans 10:17 "... faith comes from hearing the message,
and the message is heard through the word of Christ." (NIV)

My mama wears a DETECTIVE'S HAT
To encourage me to do what's right
She nudges me to make good choices
Because I am always in God's sight

Colossians 3:23 "Whatever you do, work at it with all your
heart, as working for the Lord..." (NIV)

COUPONS

ART Supplies

BEE CHORE

You are invited...

Shopping List - Groceries

CHORES

Tyler
laundry
dishes

Ryan
dishes
laundry
trash

BROOKE
dust
laundry
trash

White Rice

Brown Sugar

Powdered Sugar

Oatmeal

My mama wears a CHAUFFEUR'S HAT
Taking me places I love to go
We meet new friends and learn new things
And enjoy driving down God's road

Acts 2:28 "You have made known to me the paths of life;
you will fill me with joy in your presence." (NLT)

My mama wears a SUNHAT
When we give thanks to God each day
She says we can shine His light anywhere
Each day at work or play

Matthew 5:14 & 16 "You are the light of the world — like a city on a hilltop...."
"....let your good deeds shine out for all to see, so that
everyone will praise your heavenly Father." (NLT)

My mama wears a FIREMAN'S HAT
When my troubles seem to roar
Together we give our worries to God
And I'll soon feel blue no more

1 Peter 5:7 "Give all your worries and cares to God, for he cares about you." (NLT)

My mama wears a SHERIFF'S HAT
Helping me offer peace instead of a fight
Spurring me on to share with my brother
Cuz getting along is such a delight

Matthew 5:9 "God blesses those who work for peace,
for they will be called the children of God." (NLT)

My mama wears a DIRECTOR'S HAT
Making memories of fun-filled days
She thinks we're her favorite movie stars
As we act out silly plays

Proverbs 10:7 "The memory of the righteous will be a blessing..." (NIV)

My mama wears a FISHING HAT
When she tells us about Jesus Christ
For all her blessings she gives thanks to Him
And shares how much He's changed her life

Philemon 6 "I pray that you may be active in sharing your faith,
so that you will have a full understanding of every good thing we have in Christ." (NIV)

Portraits filled with all kinds of hats
Mama so joyfully and willingly shares
God gave them to her with His mighty love
And they're meant for others to know He cares

1 Peter 5:2 "Be shepherds of God's flock that is under your care...
eager to serve...being examples to the flock." (NIV)

Romans 12:10 "Love each other with genuine affection, and take
delight in honoring each other." (NLT)

Of all the many hats my mama wears
There's one that fits her the best
It's the CROWN OF JEWELS like Jesus wears
Cuz she makes me feel so BLESSED

Psalm 103:1 & 4 "Praise the Lord..."
"who...crowns you with love and compassion." (NIV)

And as I grow up, I'll learn from my mom
And wear MY many hats too
So I can share God's love and be like Him
In all I say and do!

Hebrews 13:7 "Remember your leaders who taught you the word of God.
Think of all the good that has come from their lives, and follow the example of their faith." (NLT)

Draw pictures or place photos here of you
and your mom wearing your favorite hats.
Write about it!
(Yes! You can write in your book!)

Talk about what you could do if you wore these hats!

About the Author

Lorie Erhard thinks the many hats a mother wears are worth celebrating!

The inspiration behind the creation of *Mama's Many Hats* came from her many adventures of motherhood, and her desire to be an encouragement to her children and to kids and moms everywhere.

She enjoys her many hats as photographer, teacher, coach, business owner, and volunteer.

She is a contributing author of *Take Out Training for Teachers* and *Give It Away Crafts for Kids*, published by Group Publishing. She lives in Central Illinois with her husband and their three children.

What do other people do when they wear these hats?

About the Illustrator

Jennifer Kalis wears many of the hats in this book, but she wears the artist's hat most often!

She is the illustrator of many books, including Gibbs Smith's *The Big Book of Girl Stuff*, *Fashion Doodles*, and *Fairy Doodles*, and American Girl's *A Smart Girl's Guide To Liking Herself - Even on the Bad Days*.

She lives and works in Central Ohio with her husband and their two children, and four guinea pigs.

Talk about what your mom does for others when she wears these hats!